Banana Man

OKELLO OCULI

BANANA MAN

Written by
Okello Oculi

ISBN: 978-978-976-148-7

Copyright © **Okello Oculi** 2019

Appreciation

This work is part of *Africa Leadership Development Project* in a Rockefeller Foundation Fellowship at Bellagio Conference Centre, near Lake Como, Italy.

Banana Man

His father called him the long man with a tall hunting stick. Mama warned bigger girls who gave him baths never to hold his "it" so that they do not catch illness of married women. His people waited for many months, including crossing a hostile river known as "dawns and sunsets that wear hunger". The millet and sorghum they planted taunted them with harsh leaves they could never cook and feed their hunger. Those who had travelled south told stories of lands with many spears of rain thrown from skies above and bushes with wet stems that give birth all year round to a row of banana fruits. They boil these fruits after peeling each and steam them wrapped in leaves as large as ears of an adult elephant.

Because they hold to raw banana fruits to peel all year round their women always brew fire inside their eyes and heat in their hips. These women cherish screams of babies each as independent as a banana fruit and the teeth that eat them.

His mother once whispered to the silence around her that her boy had the length and poison of a snake called "gobe da nisa" (tomorrow is far away).She saw a blindness in his eyes which could not see appetite, glide past and around desires, dreams, fears and fury in Zebra and man alike.

Mothers brought little children with arms broken at what her boy called "play". Her son would say in cold surprise that "we were just playing!". She had seen it in a neighbour who cut off an ear of his wife so that "she can hear me properly!". When she reached the site of his wife's scream, she found him calm as a cobra folded into a black blue heap; its head spread out, flashing a slim tongue: daring a critic to come within reach of his temper and cruel temperature.

She worried about her son with his future built around his long body and tall stick. When he beat a teacher who had slapped a little girl in his primary school - because she had very white teeth and sunlight eyes – they, that is to say government people, enrolled him as a military cadet.

Teachers turned the record around, accusing him of trying "to sex the girl". It sounded better for the image of the manhood of all male teachers. Teachers redeem heads from illiteracy and the innocence of little girls and boys whose sex is in danger. It is an easier story to retell little children who must love going to school

Military boots, baggy trousers, regular maize mash (or "posho") made him grow faster into a matching tree trunk. A rage grew under his silence about the privilege of teachers to tell lies about him and cover up voices of his classmates who told truths to parents.

He found himself walking about with folded fists and throwing punches against walls and towards clouds especially dark rainy clouds racing to cover eyes of the sun. When prying eyes of military officers reported about these muscle jerkings by him, they put his hands into a thick cloth and threw him into a boxing-gym with orders to hit hanging bags filled with sand. He would sweat wetness all over his body: like a farmer digging mounds of sweet potatoes or carrying long sack full of pressed cotton lint to fill up hollow stomachs of storage garages in cotton ginneries.

Punching hanging bags filled with silent sand did not move him from a lower class to higher ones like "beating pages of books with eyes" did. No matter how many rains of sweat fell from his body, he would win no certificates for getting jobs outside military barracks. Planting seeds of the future with fists and sweat fighting against a silent bag filled with sand was like throwing pebbles into a lake where the stones do not sprout and grow.

Military officers with clever eyes saw his growing rage and decided to dress it with a uniform. He would start doing what was called "mock-fighting" – punching into hands of a trainer. Knowing the lie told about him, they guessed that he would be fired by the feeling that he would, one day, be hitting that wicked school teacher whose sin had spoilt his life; taken him away from his classmates and put heavy military boots over his feet. He might even dream of one day being in a boxing ring with that teacher and teach the rascal a few screams under his punches.

There were reports of him waking from a dream shouting, using a favourite taunt he had learnt from Mohammed Ali: "Teacher, wicked Teacher, what is my name? What is your lie? Teacher, what is your crime?" His eyes would be red hot, bulging with rage.

The prying military eyes were careful to direct his punches away from the myth that Teachers never tell lies: do not create little prisons for locking up stubborn wills of school boys and school girls. If he breaks that myth the shadow of the teacher may be replaced by the skeleton of military officers. Colonial rule was, after all, a textile woven with many layers: from staccatos of invasion guns; sweat of mine workers in Kimberly diamond mines; and groundnut pyramids in Nigeria, to school children singing to God in English to protect their fog-dressed Queen of England. Very clever people make colonialism clever.

His mother ran in fear when one huge long man walked with thuds into her village compound. They had mangled her little boy. Here he was bringing big boots to his home where we wear soles of our feet that came to us from our Ancestors and gods. Worst of all, it made him bigger than his own father. They sent him out of school and made him a long whip. Perhaps he can become a cobra.

They have turned the head of my child, a boy I fed with my own hands. He now despises my cooking with burning wood. He claims that he saw fire and smoke inside my eyes, making them with the colour of brown soil. He says there are little red rivers running across my eyes because hot smoke from cooking fire rolls under my eyelids. He says he now knows why my mother, his grandmother, became blind because we women have been cooking without wearing cowhide across our eyes. He accused us women of destroying all the trees he grew up with, turning the land into bushes; that if we were as wise as peoples of India we would plant one billion trees each year in our country.

I was getting annoyed with him; talking and talking: like a bird at sunrise who wants to be sure that its skull and mouth open after hours of darkness, and no work. I told him that if the big boots on his feet have given him a new brain inside his head why has he not brought a pot big enough for me to collect the heat of the sun for cooking. The sun never rests after it wakes up each day. Its fire is so wide that it covers village after village after village; very generous, not dividing people by leaving some villages in darkness. Only rain can fall in some people's farms and leave other farms to roast with drought, thirst and dusts. Our sun is not a one-eyed witch. She does not teach the selfishness that some people wear with pride; and swallow to keep in their stomachs.

I told him to use his never-ending cleverness to pour the light and fire that flow from eyes of the many suns in the deeper skies into our pots. We women would mould the pots to cover over the wide grasslands on which cows and sheep and goats wander. I am tired of people who think their heads are hot with clever talk but their hands are blind cold and lazy: producing nothing for us to see and use and eat.

And I said to him that since I was born, God whispers to us every day. Just ask butter flies and birds that flout their wings on coughs by God. My cheeks are tired and creaky from blowing wind from inside my chest to raise and rouse fire under cooking pots. Why does he not use the big boots on his feet to kick wind into my cooking fire? My suffering in silence has his laziness, producing only vanity.

When my son with big boots talked about planting trees, I asked him if rain drops into his body in the military shelter where they live. The grass thatch roof he left from and returned to find me shares rain water from the sky to irrigate my sleep. If he is worried about my eyes, he should also talk about building one billion houses with roofs that respect my sleep. Bananas cover their fruits from falling spears of ran. Their lesson should also be instructions for our sons and daughters, when they wear boots.

I began to wonder about the season of laziness that has seized our lives. My father's niece had hair which collected rays of malice in hearts and mouths of people in faraway villages. When people came with illness, she could tell them that cries of people they had done evil things to have come to punish them. Her hair caught voices and thoughts like the little thing my son calls "raadioo". Why did we waste the gift in the hair of my Papa's niece? We women roasted, pounded and cooked shea-nuts for oil to drip out. We stopped at pleasing our stomach and wasted all else. The lesson banana taught of hosting alcohol, NWENGE, behind its sweetness was ignored. Where have our brains gone.

He talked endlessly about sweating in a ring and beating the head and stomach of another man who also wore a round cloth in both hands as heavy as stones. One hit on the mouth of the other man would break his teeth, crack his jaw, close his eyes with a swelling and blood rushing out from broken skin.

Each "fighter" watched with eyes of a cat to keep his body from getting hit with stones hanging from ends of two arms. Each breathes like a bull that is pulling a plough and tearing out slabs of soil: slabs as large as a banana leaf. While bulls breathe hard to feed our stomachs, my son says they beat their bodies to feed shouts by other soldier while prying eyes look on, some puffing out smoke from cigarettes held between two fingers. Some take notes and frown as two black soldiers sweat and bleed and breathe like tired bulls tilling land to grow food they will not be allowed to eat.

This practice of black bodies bashing black bodies was like other villages sending locust to our crops; four arms swinging stones to spread the gospel of what would imitate black-on-black bleeding while prying eyes puffed out smoke.

In our ancestry and what I looked forward to watch my son do – if they had not sent him to be swallowed and put into boots in the same way they put banana inside pits to ferment into NWENGE alcohol – was done with long reeds of waxy "opobo" tree. We gather mothers, sisters, fathers, uncles, aunties and girls looking for future husbands to tickle the milk in their young breasts. Rows of boys line up in two opposing teams each waving a long branch of "opobo" tree. A branch is flexible and never breaks when it lashes flesh and bones covering pride and calls to manhood.

A rule stirs inside each head and two eyes. A lash and pain must only draw a smile and a swagger. A hint of a twitch from pain evokes shame. A lash evokes eyes and waging ears of cows and young bulls expecting to be defended, protected from appetites of foreign invaders and raiders. Each smile is for stopping stampeding hooves of cattle in panic from scent of a prowling lion ended by manhood protecting the sleep of a community of owners far away from one man's solitude amid forest, bush and plain.

Each lash was an anchor for cries in babies for fresh or sour milk; in white drops sitting as testimonies to cows fulfilling a mission to ensure the continuity of humanity.

Her son had gone off the road of soldiers for promoting a community. His big boots were for growing silence under weights of elephants calling themselves "the Government". The boy who takes pride in wearing big boots now salivates when his nose tells him of meat roasted over flames or boiled inside iron pots. Metal murders the rich aroma of meat that has walked long distances and tasted many varieties of grass;

hurriedly pilfered heads of millet grain and lush leaves of sweet potatoes and green white beans.

But owners of cattle do not like eating meat. It is like cannibalism; like eating children brought up by the love of freedom by a people; eating friends with whom were shared secrets of wet grass, songs of dry leaves in seasons of drought; big bulls under whom men took shelter as furies in tropical rain joined to share our solitudes far away from a community's prayers, and indifferences of governments.

My son with big military boots denied me that moment of pride when mothers know that under that body standing in swag under lashes is a tall stick hunting for sounds of fermented banana juices and shyness of a ready girl of his age-grade. Boots that trample over the soul of motherhood bring that season of ravenous eating in locusts. They are not a banana that feeds with fruits while, like a mother, suckles her body as her body prepares for new babies. Men eat the sweet brightness of her teeth but she hides her fruits in her womb.

My son now bellows like a big dog afraid of younger loins taking a shot at climbing a bitch on heat. Our men of cattle leave roaring to the lion: convinced that too much talk and shouting takes away sharpness from blades of the brain and heart and courage.

I want my son to come back to our ways of walking through dew, thorns and rain to serve cattle and sheep and goats with caring patience in service to smiles of a community when they hear mooes of mother cows calling to their calves

His letter came from a land he called "MAU MAU" country, full of people he only knew as "enemies". I wondered if for food they drank water, millet and banana brews; if the sound of their children crying for milk, or in anger, was the same as our own; if their girls knew how that laughter we use for attracting boys; if their young warriors ate lashes of "opobo" branches to make their mothers cover the pride in their eyes so that witches could not harm them out of jealousy and spite.

He called some "prisoners" as if he was afraid to mention that they were black like him and us but did not wear boots given out by "bazungu" (his white military officers with prying eyes).

He was full of praise for one Irish officer who wanted to prove his manhood by deceiving "prisoners" to break with a hammer the head of a fellow "bad man" standing in front of him in exchange for being set free to return to his wife and children. He sweated like rain was falling on his head and followed it with a strange laughter when a victim fell down, and with wide wild eyes the killer realised that he was next in line

He liked that Irish "muzungu" as if he was the twin brother I never brought to the world, birth of my stomach. He said the practice made him think of eating rows of yellow ripe sweet bananas one by one. Each one did not know that I had just swallowed its brother; did not cry out in outrage and protest. He said he had called it the stupidity of being alone; his cousin had said it was the virtue of serving God's plan to feed birds and all of us. Birds did not own farms to grow food crops and so we grew bananas to serve them, he argued.

He said he had borrowed the practice of the Irishman, but not for killing the people of MAU MAU country. It was only to get truth out of them because they are people who love keeping secrets.

As military fighters against "these enemies" we had to know where they were hiding. They fight like cobra snakes; lying silent under a bush or inside a hole and suddenly stabbing or shooting "our men". We military people learn to become "brothers" to fight "the enemy". We asked each prisoner if his wife was young and would give him children if we set him free. We said one wicked man accused him because he wished to have his wife.

The people of MAU MAU country had very deep hearts. Talking to them was like digging for water lying under ground full of small stones. Digging a deep hole ate a lot of sweat and suffering. They never broke even if you push nails into a tongue.

Their silence is what would have pleased us his parents and sisters and aunties if he had passed the lashes of manhood at home. That memory made him angry: with envy and hate burning his chest and closing his throat.

He began to think about the power of land, of owning soil that hide bones of ancestors, of the aroma of thin smoke that come out of newly dug soil, of being a partner to cooings and shrill calls of birds across hill and river beds; of women walking home with cassava and yam and vegetables on their heads and babies wrapped on their backs. It is all this geography of life that made these people bear pain without begging for mercy.

In his fury he would hear echoes of his father calling him a "long man with a tall stick". At those times a cloud of madness would fill his head; make him grab their "stick", lay it on the table and hack it with a "panga"/machete. He later said "I would be trembling and sweating, my eyes almost bursting".

Stories he told before going "to fight" in MAU MAU country did not prepare me for these tales "from the war". He had talked of being taken before the sun came out from under the ground and commanded to enter and cross water smelling of human dung, rotting meat, dead dogs and even babies thrown there by wives who had been going with men who are not their husbands. This is what they had to do if the enemy was on the other side and waiting for them to travel on good roads and bushes.

He had also talked of being asked to kill a bull by breaking its neck with his bare hands. He, whose people are related to bulls, heifers, cows with udders round and blobbing full with milk, bulls with high humps and walk with swagger, was now talking shamelessly about breaking necks of bulls with his empty hands. His feet would be inside those big boots they put them in like raw cassava lying in soil and waiting to rot.

Those officers with prying eyes of pythons had also told war stories about using sharp spears melted on guns to cut bellies of pregnant women open and calling on babies inside them to greet them and laugh the way happy babies do. He had told of grabbing babies from their mother's breasts and bashing their heads against walls to teach them the punishment for singing MAU MAU songs about "UHURU" (or what they muttered as "independence"). In a place called Burma they told stories about black people eating people they kill at war and "drinking their blood's so that their spirits cannot trouble them since they have become 'blood brother' ".

I had often cooked him blood we shoot out by putting a piece of hot iron into veins on necks of big cows. But we never touched human blood. Blood hosts the fate of a woman and a man. To spoil it is to pour away history; to block the road of the future. Me and his Papa had taught him this wisdom but they had put his legs inside big boots which blocked words from ancestral soil reaching his head and his heart. They had locked him inside an iron bucket through which no ancestral water can find the many small holes and windows of his soles. They say it takes very thick cowhide wrapped around our heads to stop myths and legends from other lands and ours too, stealing in and blocking our lives.

I was his mother at an age measured by the tiny bulges as high as soil bulged by a rising mushroom. No one dared to call me what I was – a child. When a man came and asked that I become the wife of his son, my parents experienced a revulsion which turned into a panic. Somebody out there was already seeing me as a sensual pot. If this interest also came from one of my uncles – my mother's relatives who had free access to our home and play with her children – their sacred "nieces" supposedly protected by a taboo – the pregnancy would bring an extra mouth to be fed by them. And if a taboo became a scandal, a moment of shame, no one else would marry their daughter. I had to be deported, as it were, to be a responsibility in another home.

I did not hear any talk about being sent to school. My mother was too timid to add my name to those of boys my Papa always worried about paying for their school fees. When her husband's ears were not near she would say to me "when you become big do not do my mistake of leaving your girls at home. They say that girls who work and earn salaries always send money to support their parents. Boys claim that they are feeding their own family even if they spend money on alcohol and chasing mistresses. Send your girls to school; fight your husband for their welfare; fight the village".

"There is abomination in the land. The blood of little girls flow as men rape them under cover of marriage". I heard my mother singing those words as she peeled bananas for a meal in the home. She was bitter about the pain when her husband first "took" her. She remembered old women waving a white cloth with her blood stains on it and dancing in celebration.
Their hawk had caught an innocent little chick whose mother hen dared not shout in protest because custom and poverty had woven cobwebs across her mouth.

She had been lucky that her mother always carried her on her back, her little legs forming a shape like two teeth of an army ant. It had made her pelvic bone grow wider and prepared them for the forced coming of her first baby's head. Less fortunate girl-mothers had suffered their sacks of urine getting torn by the head of the baby. Those with sharp mouths accused the little things of coming with evil spirits from their parents. They mocked the flow of urine out of their loins; cursing them for bringing shame to their in-laws. As they say, ignorance is cruel; a willing agent of death.

The birth of the boy with boots swallowing his feet came with a lot of pain. Her mother had warned her not to scream; to push with all the strength in her stomach. She would sweat, she would be there to hold her, wipe the sweat from her face and body. She was to look into her eyes and see a mother's love and pride in her for soon becoming a new guardian of her husband's clan and that of her parents. After her baby had left her stomach she would not be left hollow. The spirit of a grateful community would rush in to fill her, celebrate her womanhood.

Mama said she had followed what women did at local village meetings; rolling out evidence to convince people listening to them to turn their hearts and heads. Knowing that spirits of our ancestors were watching this little moment of history she kept telling me that she had been a good woman, shared food she cooked to others; shared herbs her people had taught her to cure snake bites and running stomach in children which kill little ones so easily by drying up their blood; she had been clean from desires of other men, rolling her eyes and shaking her hip for only her husband to get fumes of her body's fire. Because she had been a good woman they must protect her daughter, hold their hands around her child so that death does not hunt successfully for her baby and her body.

Each time I see the big head of the boy who now wears large boots, I remembers the pain that shouted from between my legs as he came out of my womanhood. I do not curse him; I dare not desecrate the product of my birth stomach.

I saw a twinkle of happiness in my Mama's eyes. She had with much delicacy in her glance checked the baby's navel and noticed his tiny stick. Her daughter would be praised, not mocked, for giving her husband's clan a warrior; one who would feed his people, dance with vigour and grace to seduce a beautiful girl that will ensure the good looks of their boys and glaring beauty of their girls in order to compete for and bring a crowd of cattle to claim her eyes; and white sparkle in her teeth.

She said to make a strong man out of the baby, I should after twelve moons had passed, start delaying his sucking the breast and let him cry until his Papa shouts in protest. Let him scream to know that even rain ignores hunger in baby banana fruits. Lift him with one hand so that he dangles like a cassava root so that he gets a taste of physical danger. When he gets to be four, shout and slap him and twist his ear and insist that he must not cry. Show him power to teach him the taste of a harsh world waiting for him out in the geography of life. To see her spoiling him later as grandmother, calling him "my husband" would puzzle me. As they say, if you want to give your in-laws a goat, let them take the rope from your hand, and hear the struggle hidden in its hooves.

The last letter from him in what he called "MAU MAU Country" made my stomach feel as if pepper hidden inside a ball of MATOKE had burst walls holding it and was roaring all over walls of my stomach. They had turned my boy into a butcher.

Where was the boy who had defended a little girl in a school classroom; the defender of the weak in serving fumes of justice inside his little boy's head?. He had allowed himself to be infected by the beast in an Irish officer who desired and longed to show his English bosses that he too was capable of being a brute; not being too soft to defend the British empire, the Queen's cannibal in a colony.

He told a story from "MAU MAU War" about hiding in a forest, rain falling on leaves and then on them; birds and insects cutting a wet silence and darkness. Light from a moon whose eye rain clouds covered and went away from. The moon is very stubborn. It refused to be closed by those rolling clouds.

In those moments of clear shine from the moon he saw a cobweb hanging from ropes linked to leaves in four corners. In its centre an insect struggled to take its future away, yet each shaking looked weaker as if struggle led not to freedom but a beckoning surrender and death.

A little insect had from within its belly rolled out strings, attached them to leaves to hold and be witnesses to his hunt; rolled some in circles in the same way we women weave baskets with leaves of palm plant. From each of us, he began to think, there are strings and ropes to be rolled out for hunting. Even the smallest person has wires of thin ropes stronger than a human body since no one can hang like those wires in sun or rain, in rainstorm. Perhaps that was inside those MAU

MAU fighters; ropes for building their road back to land they called their heritage. Perhaps words used by their prophet called "KIMATHI" were as strong as strings rolled out by spiders from their stomachs.

A spider had crawled swiftly towards the struggling insect and started sucking its insides. Like a flash of lightening across the rain enveloping them, images came back to him of a man made of chalk stretched out on a small cross inside the church in their school. Perhaps the soldiers who used a spear to jab holy blood out of him were looking for his liver and kidney for a ritual. The Irish soldier had told him about men of power in his country who meet secretly at night in secret locations to share roasted liver and kidney of young boys to drain out new power. Those who became members were to increase their wealth and to climb up high political hills.

He kept telling people who came to hear and know and perhaps believe that these "enemies" in MAU MAU country had one bad disease, an illness of the mouth which his officers with peering eyes called "DEMOKATI" or "DEMO". It was passed from mouth to ear to mouth and ear till everyone started shouting bad roars like chicken that had seen a python or a wild cat.

One of them said that in their country it was a disease of cattle called "foot and mouth" disease. It rots mouths and heads of cows. It eats like clouds of locust falling on farms-eating food crops from leaf to stem; leaving only memories of all the sweat, all the sacrifices, the fire of son on backs of farmers. It makes men cry openly even when women are near them.

In MAU MAU country they talked like mad people; shouting about taking government from foreigners as if babies cry out from leaving the womb in the morning and shouting wisdom and instruction to mothers and elders at sunset. As if babies can cut firewood, start fires for cooking, cut and peel bananas; catch and pluck and chop-up chicken and 'make stew with raw groundnut paste and salt and pepper'; and blow-up flames with their mouths and fill their eyes and weep from stings of smoke and feed a family and all our relative and neighbours and visitors. Government cannot be done by babies innocent of appetites of power.

Babies must pee pee and poo poo and roll their eyes with enjoyment of the warm milk of mothers rolling down their throat and around their stomachs; notice mothers walking away and about like trees and discover that they must crawl on their little hands and knees before they too can dance by stamping on soil and grass instead of bopping up and down from mother's back.

We soldiers, he would say, know that not every hand can fire a gun. The sound of a gun shooting out of its mouth or nostril can frighten a new recruit. The sound of the voice of a child shouting orders to elders must create fear. When I was chosen to play the game of "catch-throw-run and cross a line" – they call it "RUGBI" – I could see fear in the eyes of white players in teams facing us. It was fear of one who should be accepting and obeying orders; one who should be kicked and slapped and hit with buts of a gun now facing a "master" eyeballs-to-eyeballs.

He was, he told silent ears but open mouths, that he played the game of bashing bodies of European soldiers to stop them from running with a ball, grabbing that ball from off their hands; hearing one groan when he hit them hard. If he held the banana and eggs between their buttocks he would hear a scream of pain. He enjoyed those times. It made him understand the fear his officers had for "DEMOCRATI" in mouths of MAU MAU enemies; fear of eating food cooked by a leper.

He would say that "RUGBI" taught him that all men are created strong and weak; full of courage and fear; blessed with a taste for victory from breaking bones in others. A fire filled the body when chasing to catch, block and bash an opponent. A kind of satisfaction filled his throat when teeth and blood flew out of the mouth of a 'victim' he had "tackled".

At those moments he wished that he had hit the school teacher with a "RUGBI tackle". It crossed his thought. It was salted with stories told by elders at beer-drinking revelries: of seeing Europeans bleeding from wounds cut by spears or arrows as our people fought them years past. The wild-eyed MAU MAU "enemies" always sung that "red colour" will bleed and wash the eye of the sun at dawn.

Their song for blood always made him remember that if he had not been sucked into becoming a soldier he would have shed the blood of a lion or an elephant to gain a higher manhood than that of showing no fear of a hissing stick landing on one's ribs as girls and mothers looked on with many feelings and wishes. The MAU MAU people did not play the game of sticks, but held young bananas between legs of boys and cut away the leaf nature used to cover its ball of fire and sensuality. Blood rolled out to award the pride of being called a 'Man'. It was their form of RUGBI used by his military officers to protect MAU MAU people from the disease of 'DEMOCRATI'.

One of his officers would say that MAU MAU "traitors" forget the African wisdom which instructs children "NOT TO TALK WHILE EATING ". Here they were eating some "civilization" from British people who came from far to help them and they were screaming and taking oaths made of eating fried goat-meat dipped in blood collected from each of their fingers; dancing with wild fiery eyes and calling out to 'DEMOCRATI' to come down from thick forests full of yelling evil mountain spirits with long thorny tails.

That officer accused European officers of destroying the good-nature of 'natives' by throwing pieces of 'education' – a little reading of letters and counting their fingers and toes in the name of feeding them with "MATHEMATICS". Those that had been carefully nurtured by their own trusted elders with tales told under moonlight were without responsibility, had been allowed to read books that reported on and even celebrated wild orgies in England and France and Germany.

These indulgences were called 'revolutions' in which heads of kings and their glorious assistants were hacked off. To native people who drink blood of their victims and eat raw liver of youths to suck into their wasted bodies the youthful vigour and powers of these unfortunate 'things', such writing made fluids inside their skulls to boil. They wrongly saw their utterances as 'enlightenment'. They should have called it the mutation of "darkness"; a poison with the subversive power of a MULLATO which ruins roots of blackness and whiteness in the heritage of children

We could see that his officers had scratched a boil growing inside his heart and head. His school report had always shouted that he was a clever child; either coming on top or among the first five ranking. His classmates sung his praise even to villages around our own. When he was captured and hauled away to military barracks, his fame sank into a silence. School Reports from his military classrooms became hidden inside the high military boots he wore when he visited. From a magnet of admiration he became an oddity wearing a vapour of terror. One former classmate coined the tag of a "SHOUTING IGNORAMUS" – hinting at what is hostile and unknown to his own people.

Perhaps his prying-eyed new owners did not want him to be hugged as their warrior in the tradition of those whose spears had been silenced by guns of foreigners. He boasted of battles against MAU MAU people who were not enemies of his people; whose war against strangers who had stolen their land and also forced them to dig soils and weed crops for them was hidden from their ears.

 Each time he rolled out stories of bravery and narrowly escaping death, women and girls did not beat ululations inside their throats; and men only made wrinkles on their foreheads taller and deeper. Old people obviously knew more about the world than him. You cannot clap with one hand and no matter how wide the hand of foreigners was, it could not cover light from coming down from the sky.

He had held on to pronouncements in his School Report. He was a clever boy. He would not allow sounds of military bugles and boots to silence it. He told of stealing entries into the "Officers' Reading Room (OOR)" and read newspapers from their home. He first liked reading about 'Rugbi' and 'DEMOCRATI'. Increasingly, he read reports about what was being done to Africa and of activities by business adventurers. He learnt that there were other companies in Africa; and met comments by foreign politicians, notably a certain "KWAME NKRUMAH" who was described as "ungrateful", "rude" and "hostile" to those who had picked him up from the bushes of the "GOLD COAST" and taught him some English with which to shout his "gibberish".

These written blows thrown at "KWAME NKRUMAH" reminded him of tackles during 'Rugbi' games. He could see in his mind this African man running with a pot full of boiling words to cross a line which would earn him 'DEMOCRATI' points. He also met names of 'AHMED BEN BELLA' in a place called 'ALGERIA' where French troops were fighting 'rebels'. Then came the name of 'PATRICE LUMUMBA' whose tongue was said to pour out words as rousing as Belgian "POLAR BEER".

The more he read, the more he realised that he was attending higher moments of learning than the mates he left in school classrooms. His education was becoming superior but the girls he wished to seduce admired only boys in school classrooms especially the few in higher colleges whose number could not match one fingers or toes. He was reading the knowledge that European officers were knowing; floating unseen in a high sky of wisdom like an eagle. He could pick his victim while floating on a chair of invisibility and silence. Only God and his ancestors were seeing him.

A growing jealousy and bitterness grew against those who waived names of colleges as badges of being cleverer and wiser. Like a root of a banana peeping out as a sampling, he also grew a sense of watching, reading motives and egos of others from high up in the sky before pouncing on them either in a kill or for manipulation. He grew the power of a warm smile, a piercing look into a target's eyes, dropping intimate information about the victim that could only have been collected from flying high in the sky, hidden from their eyes.

He would boast about his patience, his grilled memory for details like names, routes from home to other destinations, friendships and indulgence of sensualities and raw appetites, all to be used to back a smile or warmth in a throat to ensure the success of a hunt. The eagle only hunts; has no time for frills and flows of a skylark. He is economical, ensuring that a target has only one chance – that of being done in.

He has boasted of the brilliance he invests in hunts. Some people accused him of being cynical, even ruthless. They were in haste, not seeing farther than the boundary of their wishes, their farms, and their hatred for him. He had a nation to build. If a class of senior military officers had begun to regard themselves as future rulers of the country and its different provinces; not as military geniuses ending civil wars across Africa; stalemating foreign invaders ready to light fires of civil war in countries and patches rich in mineral deposits they need for their satellites, rockets and cell-phones so that they can haul them away cheaply by keeping local governments weak and communities bleeding endlessly, it was not cynical to save them from professional indignities by throwing them down from military aircrafts. That act is merely a semi-colon in a sentence of nation-building.

They spread stories about him inviting professionals to dinner at his Presidential Yatch and later feeding them to his team of crocodiles with a taste for political opponents highly endowed with naivety about matters of statecraft. He had known highly educated foreign officials working for global bodies, including the United Nations, calmly advise him to "terminate" – their softer way of saying that they be killed – and gulping down glasses of high quality alcohol to wash down their burden of thought. These men and women knew about the deliciousness and bitterness of statecraft. If our own people lacked that gift, it is not fair to curse my assistance to them in this sector of political education.

He had been ordered to burn down a village said to be "full of MAU MAU rebels" in the morning, dressed up to play a game of 'Rugbi' in the afternoon, abandoned to sit alone inside a Land Rover truck while ''my European teammates'' drenched themselves with alcohol in celebration of triumph or loss. It was my taste of blessings of power in habits of foreigners. It was my lessons in culture for feeding 'DEMOCRATI'. grass and ripe heads of millet suffer when hungry cows walk over them.

He complains that people accuse him of cowardice by listening to foreign officials who reminded him of what befell MAU MAU fighters who refused to give up fighting to win back lands of their Ancestors. The British hanged

DEDAN KIMATHI so that his fighters would lose heart following the fall of one born under sunlight at midnight. That did not give me fear. I did not throw my military courage into a banana grove to fertilize soil for groundnut seeds to open their mouths.

It was, he said, remembering advice by an elder that he that urinates on himself as rain is falling on him will not know shame. People will not see the difference between waters from two lakes. Those who throw arms and legs at the enemy at the same time may find no place to fall and continue the fight. You cannot borrow another man's testicles to get from your wife a child who looks like you. Those who mocked me forgot that I pushed them off balance for so long that Time itself became my walking stick.

A central view in his galaxy of ideas for action is that the banana plant knows that the future of its clan does not lie in the bunch of fruits that birds and man feed on. It lies in the roots hidden under soils that sprout as samplings after her stem as a mother no longer drinks water and eats salt from roots. This had been his guiding light at midday and midnight.

This road to the future put fire in his feet, mouth; in his eyes. He knew that a row of banana fruit yellow with ripeness and boastful of its mission by spraying perfumes into winds blowing in all directions would attract hunger and greed from bats, birds, flies and man. Nature puts the virus of self-interest and survival in all including wind and sunlight. Crocodiles and mother lions hunt for wilder beasts roaming and rushing in longing for new blades of grass. Even though grasses do not hear the greed in lion and crocodile, it suffers roving jaws of wild beasts. Grass must put its trust in roots hidden from ravenous and dutiful teeth of goat and deer and zebra; and from fires lit by herders of livestock luring new shoots.

They accuse me of roving around our vast community calling out spirits of our Ancestors long dormant in a people tortured by war and hunger and drums of division. Speeches from my chest rang out to rallies of peoples in corners of a rich land; a voice that rose and dipped in melody, rage and praises. For five to six hours I washed rallies as wide as newly landed clouds of honey bees or quilla birds at a feast on grass, grain and leaves of trees; like our music.

I made them call up our Ancestors to witness a birth of a nation throwing off old and wrinkled shells of pains, bleeding and hunger for respect. Some laughed at a man with nothing better to do, a man afraid of mountains of files crafted by officials; a man starved of attendance of lessons inside classrooms and smells of chemicals bubbling in laboratories peopled by eager modern witchdoctors. Others saw an empty shell groping for vapours of intelligence from screaming crowds herded in front of him.

But I had known that it takes many rounds of rain drops to soften soil for farmers to plant crops and for crops to come up and look up and see if skies can be trusted to feed futures.

Our visitors from Europe were afraid of 'DEMOCRATI' and of fingers in our hands being at peace and dutiful to ourselves. Elders remember millions of hands falling off, hacked as barren banana stems. We raised our fingers as speeches at meetings in villages to wave agreement or to quarrel. Cutting our fingers and wrapping them on handles of hoes from sunrise to sundown on farms owned by foreigners, killed our waving our meeting of hearts and wrestling matches by minds in settling our common matters. A long season of gloom sat on our land; bringing drought to us like grey fibres taking our stem of bananas whose bunches of fruits have run their mission to bring sweetness and "MATOKE" fufu.

It was my destiny to open mouths of our women to sing again in joy, romance and arrogance. I looked at our sky at night and saw stars singing a distant charge to join them and I called out "MAKOSA" song, guitar, drum beats to yield rhymes as wide as the fiesta of stars singing across our tropical skies. We chased away morose sounds of snows and winters and screeches of machines come to droop over melodies in tropical forests and roaring rivers Nile, Niger, Congo, Zambezi and Limpopo.

Colonialism taught us that rulers eat while other mouths rot with emptiness. They taught us table manners of drying saliva inside our jaws from the aroma of boiling broth of beef or hisses of juices from thighs of antelopes and buffalo on barbecue. When I blew the flute of the hunter for our people to rush out and eat our UHURU (independence), there were shouts of planting and watering corruption. When I told party leaders to measure the distance between their navel and buttocks by bottles of beer poured into dry stomachs, they forgot that I had been taught by 'Rugbi' team mates who threw whiskies down their gullets while I crouched dutifully inside a land-rover truck. "Power must eat", they roared in wet drunken songs.

Building a people is not a single fiesta of dancing and getting wet all over. Colonialism had fought our pride for many decades, longer than rings on tusks of bull elephants. Rousing them up the week after UHURU was as full of danger of being bitten as castrating a bull dog. The new freedom hated work; hated sounds from muscles sour from hippo lashes on backs; of sighs of wives and daughters mending aching manhood in men; and parenting.

I also learnt the lesson of lions; it takes skill, cunning and hard chase to catch a buffalo for a meal. It takes putting nostrils on waves of wind to know there is blood and meat to nag hyenas over. When alone, one only hears belches of lions and their cubs; but with a team of hungry teeth and daring and threat, it is possible to taste satisfaction. My officials soon learnt that geography hides many appetites and will to catch the virus of colonialism. The hord that surged around me, and my officials in distant provinces had little thought about the hundreds of thousands of fires I had lit in rallies for building a nation. Like ravaged soldiers set on a grove of ripe bananas, their throats betrayed mates trudging along far behind.

The wise leopard kills a dear and drags it up a tree if hyenas are not to laugh her into betrayed hunger wracking her body. It was a wisdom larger than its sly frame. It reminded me of an officer telling me that Empire had a short memory. After draining his wit and grit it would throw him back home into a slum. He was taking a precaution, playing a secret card with fate by putting away some relief in a house in his home town. ''We Europeans believe in the Christian teaching that one sins alone, does not share blame for it in front of his Maker. You Africans believe in 'blood debt' by a whole clan. Perhaps it will protect you when you are away from her majesty's service. With your new habit of earning government alone, all by and to yourself, our virus may have spread. I warn you to be careful. Take it from a "MUZUNGU" or "TUBAB" or "BATURE" — whatever you call us", he had said calmly.

It was a tempting moment of kindness from one used to barking at African soldiers. With the wisdom of hyenas for hunting, the ravenous swarm around me had waited for me to strike, risk my neck; betray a boyhood friend who had believed me to be a fellow hunter in the jungle of politics for seizing UHURU. If I fall they will eat even my bones as "pepersoup".

In the end it was vast Villas I bought across Europe that were slaps on the faces of those officers with prying eyes who wiped mud under their boots over our backs and head no matter how well we had pressed them with hot steel slabs with wooden handles running over their backs so that they looked like stretched-out cats. Here I was, a carrier of UHURU, triumphant in our new politics while they rotted as I discarded dregs of empire. I could employ a private eye to find them out and invite them for "dinner" in my villas.

Those I had hit really hard in those 'Rugbi' tackles are probably dead or coughing with porous lungs. Life is wicked. It had been so for us. As if God was so angry with the Black Pharaohs who had travelled from our Great Lakes Plateau that he sent locusts to eat not only our crops but minerals bellow them; and irrigate the savannah with our blood; and cries turned to rain clouds.

They said I stayed seated over power for too long. But building a country is like tending the growth of a child. You cannot tell her tooth to hurry up from under the empty gum; bones in the hips of a girl child to hurry up for a baby to shout his way from a womb into fresh air and isolation. A child screams out without the power of speech as a hunting spear.

Growing up takes time. The baby of a giraffe falls from a high platform, wobbles to grab a walk but it cannot kick off the malicious infanticide in a fox or hyena. And in countries like CONGO, hyenas became midwives tending the birth of UHURU. Some countries had pythons eager to swallow their freedom.

The talk of the arithmetic of roads built, schools hosting yelling children, hospitals mending ravages hawked by mosquitoes, rivers of oil trapped in barrels – to measure how many wisdom teeth our UHURU has grown. I would always ask for SOAP to wash sediments of wax left by prying eyes and colonial wits inside heads, eyes, ears, mouths and spinal cords. I know this matter well. My hand would shoot out a salute without my permission if those military officers were to enter my villas in Europe and Morocco. It takes time for blood to dry up.

I tried washing souls of a people. Some things were done in revenge like calming the rage in me from seeing youths with bulging muscles sweat roaring down their necks and backs as they carried a railway engine across a river – their puffing becoming a bridge. Ordering European businessmen to carry me on their shoulders as I sat on a raft, was a weaker sting than the bite of a mosquito distributing malaria. Telling our people that God still remembers names our Ancestors called on her to bless us - before Christian messengers brought their own - was heard with thrills by many but with panic by some.

I watched with joy as those who had been cooked by schools wriggled and twisted with confusion when grandparents dug up names from old pots. Alien names had grown into their skins with ancient ones smelling with the rudeness of Sulphur Dioxide inside school chemistry laboratories. It was like vehicle mechanics struggling to turn their suit stained work clothes into white coats used by medical doctors and nurses. Stains in a brain are hard to scrub out. I was told of a female foreign student in an America University shouting in horror when a white worker climbed out of a hole in the street she was walking on. He was coated in red mud and adorned a yellow iron head cap. In her southern African country only her kind of people did dirty work as employment. She could have been my victim of name-changing as a plough for farming a new country. She could have been in my classroom when I slapped a white missionary teacher in defence of justice for a little girl.

Foreign cumulus clouds swooped down over my head when I turned the game of changing personal names to that of owners of farms; owners of transport buses and trading companies, and owners of mortuaries, mines and skies above hotels. Building a country was not a time for changing names in that manner and over such matters. So I was told in loud newspaper headlines, I felt excited to see my photograph on their newspapers.

Whenever a secretary asked to open a call by a president of an important country who I suspected was calling to warn or complain or order a termination of my baptism by ownership, a thrill rushed through me. It recalled those moments during games of 'Rugbi' when an officer was running with the ball and came under my orbit for a tackle or in my wish for a smashing. I would salivate and take aim. I always made a hit. Coming from a tall and big body, my targets would say later, that it felt like a whip with a trunk of an elephant.

I would say calmly that my people felt that companies or business people from the particular country had "eaten enough from our pot". They say that the child who secretly steals meat from a pot will one day learn that his hand had grown so big that it can no longer come out of the pot and his mother would catch him pot-handed.

They would protest at my use of the word "steal" and I would replace it with "liberate". Their media would put fire into the affair by claiming that I had called the president a thief. Then they turned the tip and blade of spears at me, counting numbers of my villas and flags of my freedom and new superiority over officers with prying eyes.

Those officers with prying eyes were clever, thinking people who were always looking at us with eyes of a cobra which sees with their ever active tongue. They planted their eyes and ears on the bushes we walked across. By the time they could hear our speeches, it is as if our dreams as we slept flowed to them.

Just as we kill chicken and goats and cattle by putting sharp knives over ropes inside their necks so that blood would shoot out, they drained our anger for fighting by cutting off heads of our strong men and women with power over people. In our MAU MAU war, it was said that they tied a rope round his neck and pulled the rope around a bar of wood. As his chest rose for breadth they fired many guns with bullets which could resist the shield of pride and courage and warriorhood and contempt which flowed like a smoke around his body.

They had been told that a ritual was done in a banana grove: wide and wet leaves shining and singing with each drop of rain falling on them being a witness. First a white cock, then a white goat, with two bells hanging from under its neck, had cried out on scenting human appetites and will for their blood and flesh. White was the colour of death and of the theft of their security in farming crops and grazing animals; leaving their lives limp like ashes. This power in Dedan Kimathi had to be burst and drained out with the use of an alien fire; a fire whose ritual incantations were inside churches far away from these tropical forests and fertile hills.

They shouted and strutted about with a hollow pride of conquest, a stubborn belief in fire for cooking Africa inside their heads. We looked at their self celebration and smiled to our silences.

On looking a little closer, we sat around fire at military camps and respected their skill as butchers. Just as they did at home when cutting up a goat, we killed their yell of fear and protest to be certain that other animals did not rush out for a war. We then cut through sheets of flesh which held front and hind legs to the trunk. The head was severed and thrown into a fire to cover staring eyes hinting at guilt we were unwilling to talk about.

They had licked their wounds from battles against two kingdoms united against them; thrown blankets filled with small pox germs to mow down a stubborn population; and thrown rinderpest at their cattle to make common meals of meat and milk rot on fallen bones and sunken skins drying under tropical sun. To the kingdom that saw death and desolation in a partner and quickly talked wishes for peace, they gave reward of territory carved and yanked off from the other. Betrayal became a wall pulling two patriotisms away from a history of martial dances of brotherhood. The officers with prying eyes looked on and picked their teeth from buffalo meat roasted at a picnic.

They were relentless: falling and drizzling on us like our tropical rains when farmers longed for crops to grow. For rain they built schools. Just as banana groves drink many months of rain for them to flower and sprout rows of fruit, they planted more schools for farming minds amid dense banana leaves. In dry lands where millet and rice, sorghum and yam grow in a hurry and farmers rest at the coming of seasons of drought, they planted few schools.

In moments of cheeky wits, officers with prying eyes would tell us during drills that those who live on bananas grow weak knees and hearts that tremble with fear at the belch of enemy guns. Without rain, banana stems wilt and become threads. Banana fruits get soft and rush to rot. Millet seeds remain dry and hard resembling bullets and pellets. Those who grow up eating millet or tubers store hardness inside their knees; their hearts grow hot and hard at the roar of enemy rockets. That, they would often say to us, is why they kept out of their fighting forces those bred on banana fruits. That softness, the mushiness revolted their own warrior spirit.

On hearing them, we would laugh with them while smiling in memory of stories and riddles old women had told us. I always liked the one which says "which animal is it which, if you spear it at a distance, it comes to die under your feet?". The big girls would always be the first to shout out the answer: "URINE", and we would mock at them and shout back: "How do you know?"

These officers were always telling stories which kept on opening up lids over our wits against them. But we came to see that farming minds was like growing bananas: always needing rain for new stems to flower and fruit. They were growing the bananas and we were the fruits. It was not nice thinking of fellow soldiers who died in battle as ripe bananas that had gone into appetites inside prying eyes.

Listening to their stories and chewing them together with maize or meat we were roasting over open fires in the bush, made us open windows into thoughts and designs by our Ancestors. Even simple things like a young boy climbing up a hill of manhood by eating whips from a dry stick with the bark taken off, without waving an eyelid or pinching his smile with a flick of pain had a deeper pot of honey hidden under it.

I liked beatings of a drum to match long footprints of our sun across a clean sky or of rain to accompany our night's journey across a night soft as flapping of wings of a butterfly. Lingala muzic uses song drum and guitar to hold into our bodies four seasons of our being a baby; growing into a teenager; carrying the log of parenthood and going from fire into ashes of old age. A tune should know no end, just roll on and on, rising in bumps and leaps like a roll of rain towards roaring thunder, claps and bolts of lightning and limping into a drizzle. Chicken and birds love to find their beaks and voices when a drizzle crawls into an end. Swarms of winged ants rush out to meet their willing beaks.

Those who invent those drum-beats help us to know that hearts inside our chests also know no end; working and thumping in our deafness and ingratitude at the labour they carry for our earlobes and little toes to stay on us. Those officers with prying eyes panic at sounds of drumbeats crossing a tropical night, laughing with a tropical sunlight. They stumble and jump about when daring to dance. We always struggled to hide our laughter at them; at seeing their moment of weakness, the crack in their wall.

These reflections always come to me. They urged me to be an inventor, a carpenter talking to wood; a blacksmith looking for the hoe inside his eyes, a woman throwing her genius at a rod of cassava and fire to pull out a grain that sings with water when it comes to her cold or hissing with boiling. There is also her worship for the pyramid in her memory by coating wet powder of beans with banana leaves and dipping it in boiling water as if hinting at mummies laid inside a pyramid for a journey to another life. ''Moi Moi'' gives life. It kills to feed life.

These rich footprints of inventing our living came to me as embracing destruction, breaking stems of trees, hacking and burning soil to bring out bricks: all in the search for new furniture and shelter. I asked myself how to use poverty to start fires that would burn down habits of crawling and fawning to others. Our people know that poverty stops them from shouting at thieves who then laugh at them for remaining silent. They have walked their little daughters into chambers of rape for bowls of powdered cassava or beans to bribe empty stomachs in other children. I had known poverty has a raw sense of humour. I wished to use it to fight it; even allow myself to use it to bring freedom to those who ate it as an inherited diet.

One road was to hold as a whipping stick appetites in rich people to encourage them to join poor people in crying to different heavens to carry away their pain; to make rain fall on their farms of hope and make beans grow seeds of pride.

My Grandmother used to tell us how the banana hides its children from the teeth of humans and birds who eat her fruits believing that they had killed her seeds; and resembled rows of teeth of humans to mock their appetite for killing: killing cattle, killing sheep, killing chicken and even ostriches, killing cabbages and roots of carrots. Cassava and potatoes turned to using their stems to get new shoots even if their tubers are killed with fire inside cooking pots or by roasting on open racks.

The cry of babies on coming out into the world is thought to be for fear of getting killed whereas it is a moment of protest and will for combat against rupture from solidarity; from sharing food and mood with a mother; rejecting a plunge into solitude and wandering across passionate kisses and harsh hisses. Grandmother would breathe deeply at those moments, rub her face and count rows of wrinkles on her face: asking if we knew what spices she had hidden inside what looked to us like ropes from one ear to another ear. She would laugh when we jumped up to touch them, shouting many questions at her.

I have liked the wisdom of bananas in giving man and bird sweet fruits while she hid the growth of her babies inside roots that held pregnancies in a warm secret with soils and worms and termites in them. Thoughts and plans must often be hidden from the greedy teeth of humans. I have wished to hide the power in our women inside my mouth as my teeth to chew away nets of poverty and fears in men that chain them in the same way they stretch out fresh hide of cattle and drive sticks through their four corners for sunlight and heat to drink juices and fluids out of them. Our women live as dry hides, their talents for Geometry and Chemistry and Architecture rotted. Their skills for clapping hockey sticks with opponents from lands where talents of women are not tossed into dessert sands. We leave them like husks we have beaten grain out of; wiry in body like banana stems who have given us scopes for fruits.

I stay awake fanning the light in my soul with building that courage which flowed out of that new Hannibal of Tunisia; born-again son of Carthage Bourghiba. I jump and flex muscles in my will to pounce on guardians of prison gates mashing our women in the same way brewers jump up and down on ripe fermented bananas to squeeze out alcohol. When I see housewives gathered around a mound of millet straws and whacking at them to force out grains for grinding into power, I see where their jailers learn their wicked craft from.

I started education camps for free women to wash out of minds prison locks on teenage girls, locks whose weight are already making their necks loop like stalks holding ripe sorghum tassels; locks whose terrible holds make horrified mothers throw in their own clangs in screaming at daughters not to run into public markets and sing out names of fathers and uncles and cousins who have raped her and her sisters and their playmates. Bourghiba did it and lightening did not strike him dead as guilty men of religion promised him as reward for abusing gods. I would do it, but carefully.

Men with religion as fishing hooks on their tongues would proclaim my liberation camps as harems, assemblies for sex orgies by politicians and my loyal supporters. They themselves would dress up like witchdoctors to do rape raids and later weep for honour during sermons: rousing fathers and true believers to defend honour by burning down my residence and parliaments as putrid lakes of orgasm and warfare against good souls and self-respect of all.

My wife rushed out with more courage than all those grabbing money from busy-body foreign diplomats claiming to protect 'human rights' – not rights of goats and rams that are slaughtered to benefit throats of foreign tourists and those who believe that they can make women suffer here on earth but bribe God to give them wealth and power over other oppressors of women.

She talked about talking for poor women. After hearing stories about snakes that have taste for biting women that wear sweet perfumes, she and her platoon of women would talk only at places where her stock of anti-snake poison would still cure her leg better than Bitter Kola liquid.

Men of religion were quick to mock her as the promoter of fancy architectures of headties. But they were afraid; frightened that she would pick wax gates from wits of women who would become richer than men in towns and villages. She was not as daring as Bourghiba who poured out education to wash cooking smoke and bites of hot red pepper from eyes of women by making them medical doctors, lawyers, airline pilots. The dawn of women medical doctors shooting needles into buttocks of men who are not their husbands; of women medical doctors getting qualifications on knowledge about the nudity of men, had made Tunisia rumble with rage and panic in men.

But that brave man did not halt. He would haul men of religion and secretly elated old women to the airport to watch aeroplanes with women as pilots roll and fly up with big noise, or come down and touch earth again like pigeons and ducks bobbing up and down on waves of the Mediterranean Sea, and hold their mouths in wonder. Those who had no money to buy airline tickets to go to strange lands would say loudly: "I will never fly in that thing if a woman is controlling it!" Old women would laugh and wish they were still young like those fortunate women pilots.

Such new borders of wishes would come to be only if I kept power tightly in my hands while when sleeping or while watching my eyes staying actively and safely open. In our times one had to be sure of which music the radio did broadcast at dawn; whose voice rolled out what kind of news. Those military officers with prying eyes had always told us not to trust men with no training in responding to military drills; men with no lungs for making crickets jump on parade ground with calls for forward match and salute and "eyes-left"; "eyes-right" and "stand at ease". They would say such men have no stomach when trouble comes, they would start inside their pants their own River Niger, Congo River or River Nile when a gun pops under their feet.

The secret of bananas in protecting the continuity of one's family line is never to put trust in appetites of humans and birds. Shea butter trees put sweetness to cover a hard shell over nut for a seedling to eat. Sweet sour-sap uses thorns over a bitter sheet which covers a sweet sponge that cuddles stone-hard shells over germination nut just like white lumen round yoke under shell of an egg. They are all weapons for fighting the war against lack of trust in appetites of those seduced into the mission of broadcasting that song of fertility and continuation of family lines. Some of those seduced may find gain in ending the line of fertility like those who roast, pound and drag oil and cosmetics out of shea-butter nuts and make omelette out of fertility in mother hens. The matter of trust is expressed in that saying by old women that the bird that wants to fly must first open its mouth wide for a mother bird to put flesh of fish into it. Those who miss what comes out of mother's mouth wilt into starvation inside or around the nest. The loyalty of a mother's mouth may skip some anxious beaks.

This matter of loyalty has over long years past been ensured by those against whom I have to protect my power. Their secret was in imitating the spider; its fecundity in rolling out thin threads harder than steel and criss-crossing them into a sheet, a web for hunting winged ants and flies. Each thread of saliva plays its mission as a soldier in Spider's mission, holding tight to its link to other threads, other knots and silent elasticises of family loyalty.

For each rod of saliva they used the womb of a daughter sent out as a wife and harvester of information. They sent wombs of daughters across distances both short and long. Distances were short when first cousins carried a womb to a first cousin. Just as the tapestry of a spider's web is revealed by the reflection of sunrays at dawn or by drops of water caught after a rainfall, the fly or bush mosquito that gets caught pays the price of blindness during a flight in jollity or at a mission to hook a partner for procreation.

Gossip and alerts and alarms flow from mouth to mouth among daughters and cousins and mothers and sisters and those being courted for marriage. My wife's game of rousing women united only by poverty and not a spider's web of bloodlines was no match for this architecture of loyalty. Her strength was in not being from the web and its economy of obligation to share the sugar inside her mouth with spiders tending webs. Her weakness was also that she could never hear whispers and laughter and hisses and curses and warnings and mockeries and plots against her dream.

I always told her that her women were like lone reeds of water falling from the sky. If wind did not blow them against each other they sank into soil; rolled into poodles and rivers and flood and flight. They lacked the tenacity and unity of a spider's web, its patience in waiting for victims. Poverty breeds impatience, a dispersal of vision by appetites and hunger in empty stomachs. When spiced with illiteracy among the majority of our women, speech has teeth that did not bite to draw blood enthusiasm and devotion, like small cash.

The enemy of loyalty is appetite. If I had to win the game of keeping power I had to arouse, control and feed appetites in what was called "Followers". Fela, the musical genius, had mocked appetites because it created worshippers of "follow-follow"; dimmed and silenced and roasted native intelligence inside heads of poor people; and rich people too. Each time I heard his music it was a class lesson for me.

To combat the strength of steel in spider's web, I had to weave a net with appetites. Fishermen throw out their hooks with worms rolled around them and in obedience to the fire of appetite in them, hurry to swallow steel and its sinister hook dressed in camouflage like a policeman trapping a wanted criminal.

Once at a little meal to honour the birthday of a fellow African leader, the ambassador from his country told a joke about why Christian leaders had detested a former leader because he boasted that while Jesus Christ of Nazareth had only twelve men who took notes of every word from and deed by him every moment of his staying awake, he, our leader, spent each day giving pleasures to all his favoured women turn by turn: each one, each woman according to the fire in her. That was what fathers of socialism taught their followers.

That diplomat had laughed vigorously according to the alcohol he had allowed to flow down his throat. The flow of the liquid was impossible to track since there was no space between where his head started and his chest ended. His country's independence from rule by foreigners from Europe had, as they say, been good to him. He also added that in his country, dividends of democratic governance were measured by the distance between spinal cord and the navel of a citizen. I did join him in luxurious laughter over that wit.

It struck me that there was value in putting those two jokes together. I had received a report about a young minister of finance who had been recommended to us by those who gave us a big loan. He was recruited by a big international bank from a leading university whose stock of learning was said to give very high quality wisdom and cleverness. He had been anxious to beautiful girls we had urged to benefit from his style of smiling and dancing. In his moment of elation and lush self-appraisal, he had expressed frustration over slower brains during meetings of my cabinet of ministers and permanent secretaries. The latter had been tagged "permanent and external idiots".

In a town where such jewels of conversation move with the enthusiasm of a cyclone, it was vital to tame the damage from his bad stomach. This diplomat's tongue was a moment of Grace from the Heavens.

I gave instructions to call for dinner to which all ministers and permanent secretaries were to attend together with their wives – unless a wife was under intensive treatment by all our best doctors. Each wife was to dress in her people's ceremonial garment and ornaments. I had whispered the command to a waiter while the diplomat went out to wash sweat from his face. I also instructed that the minister of finance and the top most permanent secretary must wait to be driven from their homes by one of the president's ceremonial vehicles. The vanity of my brilliant minister of finance had to be given high visibility; nurtured and honoured.

It was tempting to invite the diplomat to witness the litter of the flame of this brain wave, but it would undermine the local family hood with echoes of diplomats: those idiotic rituals much valued by our officials who call themselves "Protocol Officers". I call them witch doctors without leopard skins over their shoulders and loins to send out echoes of mysterious strength and canine appetite. It was also important to avoid lighting a bush fire of complaints by other African diplomats over missing our rare dishes and Palm Wine.

 The last time the Southern and East Africans and our Arab brothers in Algeria, Tunisia, Egypt and Morocco were here, I told them not to annoy our mosquitoes because they serve out malaria fermented in palm wine. As for Brother Gaddafi – may he come back as ombudsman of United Africa – he would demand for a tent erected for his comfort in our humid tropics.

One hears a lot of silly rituals that African leaders practice. In one country cabinet officials go down on their knees and crawl for one hundred metres before catching the much valued income of "entering the president's eyes", as they say there. In another case a German firm is reported to have built a special door which starts a song of praises and prayers for the good life of the president as ministers enter as a group to be blessed by a priest who sprinkles them with holy water to expel all evil thoughts toward the president by any one of the ministers. I rather liked that technology of a "soul fumigator" as a way of expressing the challenge of trust.

My favourite example came from Tanzania where people who take their "tea-with-bread breakfast" on a street pavement said that their leader would be the first to arrive at a cabinet meeting so that he could see which minister was developing grey hair on his/her head to know who was investing deep brain power in the job of governing a ministry.

I had to subject one of my ministers to what Jamaicans call "heavy manners" when word reached me that he would instruct his police aide to announce the arrival of "Chaka the Zulu", upon which all top officers would rush out and line up, each on her/his knees and "chin-up" so that he can inspect his own "Cowards in Honour".

To tame my Minster of Finance - the new natural genius as I nicknamed him privately - I would do something worthy of his regarding as "brilliant and inventive" – words he was reported to have used about himself.

On the day of the meal, I urged my guests to stand outside and chat among themselves, with women busying themselves with assessing each other's dresses, architecture of head ties and jewelleries peculiar to their ethnic origin, and idiocies of men colleagues. Ministers whose wives came from the same cultural zone were accused of violating the call for "national unity-in-diversity". I wanted all to see my special target arrive in ''class-and-posh", as we say about extravagant noise around oneself.

The dinner went well. Our Director of National Culture had recently done something cheeky but which secretly made me glad. He had invited all Permanent Secretaries and Heads of Parastatal Organisations to what he called a "Special Lunch" at the capital's top hotel. He urged them to order their favourite "hot drinks" and meals, including "Stake-On-The-Equator" – an invention of his for meat of Zebra, Crocodile, Buffaloes, Deers, from our Game Reserves.

While they were furiously at the meal, he slipped out, after telling the management of the hotel that each guest would pay for what they had eaten and "thrown down their threats". This was his idea of a "Cultural Coup-de-etat" to punish those who were sumptuously consuming "dividends of democracy while the poor masses were starving", he would later defend his sense of humour.

With that in mind, I told my guests not to worry about what was or was not in their wallets and "hand-bags". I joked that I had sent the offending Director out to China to be sure that he would not slip out and walk back to join and pollute our family revelry.

My operatives rushed out to nightclubs and open-air drinking places where clients chose live fish to be roasted for them to use their drinks to "wash down". It was a scandal, they would say. "The President is sampling the soup prepared specially for him by the wife of the Minister of Finance. Both men have no shame. How low can this country collapse in our moral values?. How can that minister go home and face his mother and father and clan when they hear of this abomination! Give me another beer, I must drink before we all die of such a national scandal. A Minster of Finance and our President, Chei!". That official chorus flowed into the Social Media. Newspapers of the mouth went out in a storm.

I had told the driver of the "Presidential Elephant", as popular talk labelled my rather big vehicle, to take the Minister of Finance home. His wife had an emergency national assignment to do and will join him soon. He must not be taken to a hotel so that he will be home to receive his wife before long. "I did not say before dawn!" I added, to forced laughter all around. I did wish that some of the women were shocked and jealous that it was NOT they whom the "luck" had fallen on. In that moment of wicked vindictiveness, I could allow myself some flash of vanity about my looks; if not the lure of power for the sensuality of some people.

What started as a dastardly crime was turned into a legendary example of the rebirth of national manhood. My operatives mocked past leaders who were cold and weak. They quoted with much laughter a line by a writer from Uganda, Okot p'Bitek, about educated elites whose "testicles had been smashed by books!"

I had emerged as a virile hero from being a man who was a little intimidated by a young man whose learning was much respected by international donors and economic bullies. Not that I came to fear him, since he was, after all, a civilian who had never worn military boots and almost urinated on himself each time guns and rockets made not only grasshoppers but lions and elephants run in all directions.

When I saw a Hollywood film in which an Arab man proposed sodomy to an American businessman who wished to clinch a contract, I felt relieved that my women in my cabinet would not fear that they would be told to surrender their husbands as the prize for keeping their jobs. It also saved me from hostile lobbying by Christian Clerics and Muslim Imams in the fight among elected politicians in a new culture war over legislation about rights of "Gay" people.

I regret that my Minister of Finance became a broken man. I had to post him out of the country as an ambassador to the United Nations and Barbados, a sister country where women would flock around him for his exceptional good looks and where he would regain admiration and reputation for brilliance; and where a powerful brain has a space to serve Africa's diplomacy. Moreover, as Lucky Dube sung: "smile at those you pass on your way up; you may meet them on your way down!".

A big bird once told that – sharing food and sharing belching is "an attitude of mind". As a soldier with my feet inside my big boots, I always wondered if putting a finger into a loop and pressing it towards one's chest so that fire would belch out a bullet to blow a hole into a target was an attitude of mind. Where did my heart come into that moment? And what about the fear and sweat which turned my back wet; and the shadow of my grandmother who may not see me again to hold and turn her face away to hide her tears of happiness?. I would say to the wind that my clan must do the crying with tongue and throat and breasts now soft from the satisfaction of having completed their mission.

At those moments as we released fire and ran forward to gain better view of the enemy, I would recall lines of brown ants out on a mission to pick pieces of millet or beans or dry parts of a dead grasshopper or millipede. I wondered if that show of loyalty and family hood was their attitude of mind or an attitude of instinct or the pull of appetites. As rain fell on us under cover of silent darkness and trees content to be sucking juices and minerals from soils, these images came back to me: spreading over my body with raindrops.

It was lack of loyalty which made my Minister of Finance get drunk and single himself as having a bigger brain than other members of my cabinet and myself. He had a bad attitude of mind; he lacked the smell of appetites which kept ants travelling in a single line when going to a location of food and when carrying back with picks in their teeth or hooks. After his fall from my little punch, I resolved to build that loyalty of ants in my government.

I would talk to them in groups and in private moments of "eating of our hearts", as the saying goes. During those sessions, I would tell them to notice that colonial officials always looked thin and hungry; went around in big-wheeled vehicles to run over bushes and short anthills and across swamps. They wore short khaki; covering their legs with long woollen stockings. They took our eyes away from the burst of hills and the elegance of hilltops in our tropics. They lived in low houses with red mud tiles burnt in big fires for roofs; planting tall trees to hide those residences from our eyes. They never let us know that each of them had a house built for them at home in Europe. They covered our eyes with silent lies.

It was time for us to enjoy our geography; build our homes on tops of those hills so that our people can see that we too are enjoying our freedom.

We must build back the pride that our people keep hidden like dried smoked meat of buffaloes killed in a dangerous hunt with spears. Those foreign rulers rode bicycles, motorcycles and bush-taming trucks. They were hiding the secret wealth inside cotton and groundnuts and cocoa and coffee and metals in our soils. I stole glimpses of them in pictures I saw in newspapers and magazines in the Officers' large Common Room.

We must now show these foreigners that we too have high taste; that the milk that is sweet and smiling to the master is also liked by a house-fly; that the mosquito also likes to feed its belly with the blood we hold dear inside our bodies. Our people have dripped much sweat in decades gone by and as the lizard shows us that it not only greets the glow in flowers with its eyes but also plucks and sends it down to its stomach. We must learn to eat our land; and show it a banner flapping in the wind to fan back the pride of our peoples. We must never annoy our people by living as if we are mocking their poverty;

wearing dust over our toes like them; wearing pungent sweat like he-goats and roadside mechanics. Above all, they must not annoy my anger by not joining me in building our nation.

In private one-on-one as I clapped my eyeballs at them, I would remind them of the secret of the banana; of the genius our Ancestors passed in the blood of our women which makes them get hot with the duty to continue our race. Birds have it too. A female dog yells in anguish as she suffers suitors often tearing her blood-caked ears as males hustle to plant their seeds; watched swarms of ants mating as they flew: with female ones biting off heads of males that had made hits into them. We all must join our women in nurturing the children they give our Ancestors. Poverty kills children; so we must protect them from being swallowed by the python of hunger.

Some people say that as children, our parents always made us eat together in a group, little hands shooting fingers into a common calabash or plate to pick a ball of mashed banana or maize "posho" or pounded yam and a piece of meat.

Little ones who lose in this competitive cooperation would run crying to mothers with portions saved for healing wounded souls. But our many fingers must hold a meal together, just us each finger joins others to hold a tuber of yam or a banana bunch to carry to a mother's care and duty.

As a parent they must remember to protect children from appetites of others. As his president, as a father to each minister, I must protect each of them against carelessness, against allowing rain to fall and roll off to join a common flood without putting out a pot to collect some for use for cooking for the family. Some people may complain but I would help her/him when sunlight was not looking, if she/he pointed at a hill, houses would sprout on it like mushrooms. Mushrooms do not come out with anybody's name written on their umbrella. I would hold the pen that would write his or her name on them.

I came to learn that an appetite often surges, flaps and waves high wings like a bush fire as it chews high grass and dense leaves of trees. As it rages it is deaf to explosions of bloated stomachs of frogs and grasshopper and rodents caught into its inferno. Those who build houses with wood and grass know that if a people rise to hold each grain as clouds and hurricanes race down to whip and punish offenders, no walls of tears and wailing can hold, push back wreckage of all in the way.

Angry voices rose up to accuse me of sowing corruption on the land and raising a deluge of mud over morality; breaking legs and wings of conscience like twigs on dry savannah. They said I was swinging around sharp naked blades of power like a toddler cutting all in his way as enjoyment of newly found waves of strength not before known to be hiding inside elbows.

I appointed people to govern over government bodies and warned not to allow those with keen eyes to look inside their pockets; not to irritate my ears with cries of poverty by persons from their clan. I talked of wishing to see their cheeks and chins bulge like roots of trees teasing soil in looking for sunshine. A favourite case was of a university teacher begging to become a ruler of a province. I told him of the patience of a chameleon desiring to eat a ripe mango whose sweet aroma reached her but whose location was far.

Madam Chameleon went and bought Patience as boots for climbing. As rain, wind and darkness mocked her swagger and swing up a mango tree, up she went; changing colours along the way to deceive hawks and snakes carrying their appetites around. On reaching the top, she smiled through puffing with exhaustion. There were flies flying around a yellow fruit. They would be additional snacks. Reaching within striking distance, she rolled out sling of a tongue, picking one at a time before claiming her prize. She sat and ate that yellow ripe and juicy mango as the sky above watched her triumph.

I appointed him to govern a university. He turned to mathematics to use as Madam Chameleon had used Patience for climbing that mango tree. Each year he would allocate admission tickets to one thousand students from families in his province. After governing for eight years, he would breed favours of eight thousand families and clans. When elections were ripe he would flick his tongue and draw in a campaign team of the grateful, and a voter base of families and clans all clad in T-shirts reading "GRATITUDE".

Those gratitudes were also mine. I shared in them from standing in shadows in their hearts. My opponents called it corruption. I called it fruits of loyalty. They blamed me for ruining cultures of learning in universities. I saw it as harvesting a season of appetites working and blooming under my patience; and peace from riots and flames and intellectual furies by a generation of youths growing without horns for charging at me. For banners of "REVOLUTION" they waved those of "YOU CHOP I CHOP: GOD LOOKS AWAY!"

I worked hard at growing appetites, the whole country blooming as my plantation of silence and moral disarmament, I had grown in which, like bananas, some families bred their hold of power while many fixed their eyes on banana fruits. Some fruits were eaten when yellow and sweet; others were cut down, left to bleed its sap in sunshine and then peeled to be wrapped in banana leaves and steamed in closed pots, the flavour of cooked leaves entering the peeled rods. The breeding families knew that fruits did not sprout as seedlings when buried in the ground.

I was a dreamer, desiring loyalty from those I had planted and irrigated their appetites. If in tending this plantation trees that stood out as if they owned all the land and sky were to be felled, my will and wills of my breed would be done. To create a plantation forest and shrubs would be hacked and ploughed over. This was my mission of creativity; of serving gods by imitating their ways in moulding the world.

Some called me a lover of my own shadow; a man of pride who regarded his head as a pot full of manure; a man who grew up with big boots dragging him down and now longed to fly; a man who was forced to do drills and hear roars of voices beating him into a rigid stick and now yearned for freedom to be a witchdoctor and a sculptor fused into one body shouting out; and scheming out a new world for himself; weeping to be immortal.

Grandmothers said that when Black Pharaohs were going on a journey they would greet people with a bellow saying "KABARA SUNNU!" and they would shout back "KABARA MAFFI" with a sad joy in their voices and eyes. It was said that at the glow of the sun at dawn these chants would be heard from inside pyramids, getting loudest as the sun sat like a red-hot circle sitting on the eyelid of the horizon. The same would happen as the sun slipped away at her setting. These stories had tickled their mind as they sat near old women. They would resolve to wake up from night's sleep to catch the fireball at dawn, but always got up late, wiping eyes with backs of a right or left hand knowing from the strong light outside the door that they failed again and again.

The Pharaohs were said to be like children leaving home, calling for and wanting to carry with them all those things they had known: each food item they like, each cloth and beads put round their necks to protect them from evil eyes of bad people who wished to harm them for being small and coming from another family's home. They would want their sisters and brothers and chicken to also travel with them.

People would laugh when they asked the mango tree and the sky to also come along. Children like the oneness of things, the common togetherness of things and people.

The Pharaohs were said to travel with their favourite wife, their medicines and foods. The animals they hunted, hippos and zebras would travel in their pictures drawn on walls of their pyramid. What were not drawn were pictures of the thirty-eight judges they would meet seated with a swinging bar to weigh pimples on her shadow against a bird's feather.

At that part of the story voices of old women become low and weaker like fires on a log of wood turning into smoke before finally going grey as ash. It was as if minds of children were to catch the story and then close a door in front of it so that it would travel into their sleep and stay seated until their waking up into more days.

Talk about the three stones used to hold pots as women raised and twisted their lips to look like tops of pots came from drawings by Pharaohs- and their officers and practitioners of religion- did not interest us beyond what was inside cooking pots.

Those military officers with prying eyes were careful not to tell him later that the Geometry, the Algebra and the Arithmetic which they drove into their heads as very important for military drills, military tactics and the explosion of weapons did come from the Pharaohs those old women talked about at home. Silence was for them a weapon for running an empire.
Grandmothers also boasted about the styles they used for shaving heads of boys by leaving a little island in the middle and arranging long hair on heads of girls also came from the Pharaohs.

Married women always said such hair attracted blessing from Pharaohs who had travelled and become Gods, and whisper down blessings for women to be fertile.

He liked the feeling of sucking life and power out of those younger than him; vigorous and muscular servants; women ripe with passion like bulging green bananas racing into yellow ripeness banana fruits with ridges on them like those on an alarmed chameleon. The certainty of life on a journey to become a new sunrise gave him joy. There was that fright of standing in front of judges and seeing pictures of his activities and relations with people rolling inside eyes of thirty eight judges: each eye as wide as a football field; like stretches of a hill of green grass for cows to graze on. He hated a flash of panic which flowed across his bowels and of a shill splashing across his back like a numbing cold whip by disapproving eyes.

When he killed to serve command by an empire and earn praised by officers with prying eyes, he had the comfort of putting responsibility on them; just the way the blade of a hoe would hear cries of roots of grass and little plants and put blame on the farmer who swung and sent its sharp strike into wet soils. When he seized charge of 'After-Empire' he felt that sensation of hunters commanding bushes and wilderness to find meat to feed women, children and elders. Bushes had to be subdued and the animals and birds and pythons in them have the power in them sucked out. When a leopard or cobra or lion or warthog charged in rage, our Ancestors instructed us to terminate the explosion of power and rage in them.

Those who had teeth of their rage blunted by me had to know that "Power does pass power", as our people say. The women and children and elders had to be served. Whenever we screamed in fear when blood came out in ropes of blood from the neck of a cow or goat or sheep or chicken, elders would shout to shut us up. And threaten us with not being given meat to eat when it had been roasted on leaping fires and inside pots. Blood must flow to feed our stomachs. That lesson always came back to me when power had to put another power inside a cooking pot.

It always made me laugh when people said in horror that I tasted and swallowed blood of fallen enemies. It made me hear again voices of older people, including my older sisters, laughing at my fear of blood bled into calabashes and pots, if it was from cows, and into sand and soil and grass, if it was from necks of chickens.

I heard bulls roar as blood came out of them and death entered their bodies. Goats yelled on smelling appetites for their bodies after they are dead and silent. I was always surprised that older people did not hear such roars and yelling. I would beat my mother's thigh to tell her to hear and do something to stop death. When wives and sisters and mother and children cried, some falling to the ground and rolling on sand and grass and ash on hearing that a man had died from our power, those roars by cows and yelling by goats came again to my ears and I wondered how close we are to those animals; the many things we share. They have two eyes, we too have two ears; they wear skins and we too wear skins of many colours. They have teeth not for decoration but for serving life's lust, like us. They sleep and we too sleep. They bleed and cry. Just like we are one; from the same judges who are waiting for me to pass through their gazes.

I arrived. There was no gate; no row of judges with gazes as wide as oceans and mats of grassland on rolling land. A cloud dark as a cumulus cloud of bees rushed and rolled around me, forming a blanket as tall as my height. At first they were round like tomatoes with tails and little leaves on them; and singing in a buzz.
As I struggled to catch a look, the crowd turned from a swarm of bees to rolling eyeballs; the buzz became cries and curses.

> You killed my child
> You smashed heads of our sons
> You poured out wine from wombs of
> our daughters
> created drought of child birth
> You hacked arms off bodies
> to roast in picnics for your armies

You poured out blood to match
waters in oceans and lakes...

The swirl of layers of swarms of eyes and din of cries and curses suddenly rolled into the mouth and eyes of a woman with wrinkles as large as rows of green banana fruits. Her eyes were calm as those of a hungry lion watching a frightened deer. From the two big toes shot out two short dogs out for a brawl. Charging each at my feet, they plunged their teeth into me, drawing riverlets of bleeding.

The pain almost made me move my legs but I remembered that those being whipped or cut for manhood show no pain for other people's eyes to see. The old lady seemed pleased.

"We have shown you your own blood but not enough to match what you shed into boots round your feet from youth to manhood", she said with a voice that was low but not tired with age.

"Whenever it rained, you saw only rows of blood falling down. When others saw water for feeding their crops, you saw blood for reaping cries and sobbing hearts. With each blast of lightning and thunder you matched them with belches of guns; blooms of cotton and flowers for bees and butterflies to sow fertility churned in you craving for grenades and bombs to explode and scatter flesh and bones. Power was in your hands deaf to delicate drips of joys in hearts; to whispers of beauty inside eyes of girls in their years of teenage". She hissed with contempt mixed with pity.

"Your ears drained out voices of old women telling your elder sisters, your elder cousins to carry you on their backs because you are one of them. You unremembered old women calling you "my husband" in endearment and for irrigating your bones. You no longer heard old men calling your mother by celebrating her giving birth to a child for their clan and for trees in the village to hear you yelling when being washed with warm water; crying because you knew not how to laugh in pleasure, in fear of being returned into mother's swimming pool of pregnancy.

The stacco of guns and barking by military officers with prying eyes blocked your eyes from the music of family hood". She talked with solemn authority.

"You must return to take baths with mud the way elephants do. Learn from our elephants to protect yourself from false winds; to guard yourself from fake "fresh airs" being blown at your earlobes". She paused to see if there was light entering my eyes.

"Go and learn again that sin is not a private poison that our Ancestors gave you as your inheritance. When your blood is spilt by a stranger, all in your clan have bled. They rise up in rage and demand repayment in un-spilled blood; a child to take over your footprints.

A new talk of sinning privately has ruined our land. It is growing over the inner shadow of our people like water hyacinth plants; blocking sunlight from fish in our lakes and rivers. Private sin is stealing from pockets of our community to be washed away with soap as leaves of our community dry up. Go back and fight water hyacinth in minds and over feet in the land. When you succeed, dogs will not drill for blood in your toes".

He had landed inside his house for travel, his pyramid. As he stood facing the old woman with big wrinkles, the stream of blood from his toes was a signal for her to send the pyramid back to 'Before-After-Africa'. A tortoise rushed forward, fireflies flashing light from all its shell, eyes and its nose.

His flight down inside its shell was at a speed faster than a smile and a wish. It was outside the control of the tortoise and that was why on touching earth all four of its limbs broke, its shell cracking into shapes of broken pyramids as a signal that it would be needed for another journey into the solar forest to be crossed to reach the thirty eight judges he had not been allowed to see. A new banana had flowered as the old woman smiled her goodbye. Her fruits would show him, they said: "THE STRUGGLE

CONTINUES". They were talking about crossing the bridge from a season of blood to a season of smiles and fertility in bananas; and butterflies showing galleries of beauty on their wings to cheer and rouse songs of love in communities.